Ahulaqs
(Arrulaat)

Ahulaqs
(Arrulaat)

By DC Fidler

Published by DCFidler Publishing

2022

Ahulaqs
(Arrulaat)
A Play in Four Scenes

by DC Fidler

Script Consultants

Travis A. Teffner
Jonathan Lazzell
Melinda Amodo
Eric Wood

Rolin Amodo
Speridon Simeonoff
Florence Pestrokof

Setting

Winter 1988. Village on Kodiak Island, Alaska. The living room-kitchen area and entry vestibule of a small house owned by a Russian-descended man, Vladimir (Mir), in a small village on Kodiak Island, Alaska. There is a pot-bellied oil stove resembling most large wood stoves. The room contains a couch and an old black-and-white television with rabbit ears. In front of the couch there is a small coffee table upon which people can set their food while watching TV.

Characters

MIR: man, age 60s
WINK: boy, age 16
EDDIE: man, age 30s, state trooper
ANASTASIA: woman, age 60s or older

Props

Coffee pot on stove
Coffee cups, sugar, and canned cream
Pop-top cans of Chef-Boyardee Spaghetti
Plates, glasses, utensils
Unopened whiskey bottle with whiskey
Casserole dish wrapped in tin foil
Several blankets
Child's small squirt gun
CB radio
Binoculars for looking out window
Small safe

Notes

Although most indigenous people on Kodiak Island, Alaska
now refer to themselves as belonging to the Alutiiq Tribe,
in 1988 (the time of this play), they referred to themselves
as belonging to the Aleut Tribe, which more accurately was
the name for people living on the Aleutian Islands. Alutiiq
is actually a Russian name for the peoples of Kodiak
Island. Prior to the Russian invasion, people on Kodiak
Island were known by their ancestral name, Sugpiaq,
meaning, "real human being."

Alutiiq Translations

Arrula'aq (Ahulaq) (ä-hōō-läk): Bigfoot-like creature
Cama'i (chä-mī): Hello
Quyanaa (koi-äh-nä): Thank you
Uutuk (ōō-dək): Sea urchin
Qilimaq: Ring finger
Taquka'aq (tä-qu-kä'aq): Brown bear
Appa (äh-päh): Grandfather
Mooqtuk (mōōk-tək): Food made from whale skin and
  blubber – In this play, mooqtuk is used as a nickname.
Alaciq (ä-lä-jik): Fried bread similar to funnel cakes

Note: "Ahulaq" is a spelling created by the author and the
  consulting Alutiiq villagers to help non-Alutiiq-speaking
  actors with pronunciation, choosing pronunciation
  common to visitors and different from fluent Alutiiq
  speakers. This distorted spelling is used throughout the
  play. Similar to numerous non-English languages, many
  letter combinations in the Alutiiq language represent
  sounds that do not exist in the English language. The
  official spellings of "Ahulaq" are "arrula'aq," "arula'aq,"
  or "aula'aq" for the singular form, and "arrulaat" for the
  plural form. The word refers to a bigfoot-like creature,
  but the literal meaning is "runaway." Spellings were
  obtained from *A Conversational Dictionary of Kodiak
  Alutiiq*, complied by Jeff Leer for the Alaska Native
  Language Center at the University of Alaska-Fairbanks,
  following a 1978 workshop in Kodiak with Alutiiq
  representatives from the villages of Old Harbor, Akhiok,
  Karluk, Larsen Bay, and Port Lions.

Premier Production

Ahulaqs premiered at Akhiok School in Akhiok, Alaska on March 8, 2012 at the Alutiiq Festival Week.

Cast

Mir: DC Fidler
Wink: Travis Teffner
Eddie: Eric Wood
Anastasia: Melinda Amodo

Directed by DC Fidler

Note About Premier

In March 2012, amidst record-setting cold and snow accumulation on Kodiak Island, after watching a production of DC Fidler's play *Boogieban*, the people of Akhiok requested for him to write a fictional play that took place in their village. The play was written in three days and staged as a script-in-hand production. The play was well received, and villagers enjoyed hearing their names mentioned in CB radio transmissions, capturing the style of village life earlier in 1988, the first winter DC Fidler visited their village. The main characters and village are fictional names. Speech, actions, and events are created from the imagination of the author.

Ahulaqs
Scene One

Setting: A winter day in 1988. Living room-kitchen area of Mir's house.

(Audio: Artic wind howls outside)

(Lights: Begin in black and fade in after several seconds of wind)

(MIR is sitting in chair watching TV weather report, emptying a can of spaghetti onto plate)

(Audio: CB: Grandma Phyllis: "Willie. David. This is Grandma Phyllis. Come home for lunch. I'm out.")

(EDDIE and WINK enter outside door into vestibule. EDDIE knocks on inner door.)

MIR: *(Muting TV with remote)* What da'ya want?

(Audio: Winds slowly fades to silence as actors talk throughout first minutes)

EDDIE: Mr. Ivanov? It's Trooper Caulfield, sir.

MIR: *(Mumbling)* Trooper my ass. *(Smirking and then yelling)* What kind of trooper?

EDDIE: State Trooper Edward Caulfield, sir.

MIR: *(Yelling)* A government agent? A flag man?

EDDIE: May we come in, sir? Please sir?

MIR: *(Mumbling)* Door ain't locked.

EDDIE: Pardon me, sir?

MIR: *(Yells)* I said door ain't locked. No damn house in the village locks their doors. Would be rude.

EDDIE: We're not from the village, sir.

MIR: Then you can't come in.

(EDDIE knocks on door)

MIR: Damn it!

EDDIE: We can't enter without official permission, sir. Protocol.

MIR: I don't honor protocol. Who's with you?

EDDIE: Your grandson.

MIR: I ain't got a grandson.

EDDIE: I mailed you his papers.

MIR: I don't open government-looking mail.

    (EDDIE whispers in WINK'S ear)

MIR: Quit whispering in my vestibule!

EDDIE: Vestibule?

MIR: Vestibule, Kelly door, corridor, boot room, coat room. Vestibule!

WINK: Grandpa?

MIR: Who's that?

WINK: Wink.

MIR: What hell kind of name is, "Wink?"

WINK: What hell kind of name is, Mir?

MIR: Who told you my name was Mir?

EDDIE: I did, sir. Short for Vladimir, sir.

MIR: Call me, "sir" one more time, and I'll whip your ass.

    (EDDIE whispers in WINK'S ear)

WINK: May we come in, Grandpa? *(Pause)* Mir?

MIR: You two ain't going away, is you?

EDDIE: I got orders sir, to leave Wink—I mean Robert— with you.

MIR: Now his name's Robert?

EDDIE: His official name on his papers: Robert.

MIR: How in hell can I be kin to a Robert? My family got Russian names.

EDDIE: It says on these papers, Robert Lewis—

MIR: —I don't care what papers say. I ain't got no grandson. No granddaughter. No son. No daughter. No wife. Ain't desiring friends. Clear outta my vestibule.

WINK: Robert's an English name. Like Mary or William.

MIR: Mary and William was Scotts. I ain't got no English offspring. Or Irish. Or German. Or Pilipino. Or Martian.

(Audio: CB: Grandma Phyllis) "Willie. David. Last time I'm calling you guys for lunch. I'll feed it to the bears. I'm out.")

WINK: I'm hungry, sir.

MIR: Trooper didn't feed ya?

WINK: No sir.

MIR: This ain't no diner. People hook or shoot their food out here.

WINK: What are you eating?

MIR: None of your business.

WINK: Don't smell like fish or bear.

MIR: Spaghetti! Out of a Chef-Boyardee can. Paid for with my own subsistence check.

WINK: What check?

MIR: God almighty. You ain't got a clue about Aleut villages, do ya? Three days out here and you'll be dead.

WINK: Aloo what?

MIR: Aleut. Aleut. The tribe you would be from if you was my grandson. The tribe what would name you a Aleut name.

WINK: Vladimir don't sound Aloo, Aloo—

MIR: —Aleut. Aleut. A-L-E-U-T. Aleut.

WINK: Let me get my writing pad.

MIR: For Christ's sake. Get in here. Both of ya.

WINK: You won't shoot us, will you?

MIR: Maybe stab you with my spaghetti spoon. Make sure the outer door is closed before you open the inner door! Don't need snow blowing everywhere.

(EDDIE opens inner door. WINK walks in first, followed by EDDIE,)

WINK: Thank you, sir. *(Mumbling)* Grand—

MIR: —Don't! Don't never call me Grand … that. Got me?

WINK: Yes sir.

MIR: I mean it to high heaven.

WINK: I won't, sir.

(MIR gives WINK a dirty eye)

MIR: You don't look like me.

(Audio: CB: David: "Grandma Phyllis? This is David. We ate at Luba's. I'm out.")

(Audio: CB: Grandma Phyllis: "Thanks for not letting me know. I'll toss it in the dump for the bears. I'm out."

(WINK shrugs)

MIR: Nothing like me or family folk.

WINK: Can't help what I look like.

MIR: Don't look like no one from the village.

(WINK shrugs)

MIR: Where did you come from?

WINK: Arizona. Tucson. Near Tucson.

MIR: Before "near Tucson."

WINK: Las Vegas.

MIR: Before that.

WINK: Los Angeles.

MIR: How long's this go on?

WINK: Foster homes. Church schools.

MIR: Jail?

WINK: A couple times.

MIR: Psych wards, crazy places?

WINK: Once.

MIR: Once?

WINK: Three times.

MIR: Cause you was crazy?

WINK: Evals.

MIR: Cause you was crazy.

WINK: No sir. I mean no.

MIR: Why was you sent up here to the middle of nowhere?

WINK: Gangs.

MIR: What kind of gangs?

WINK: Crips.

MIR: Like Mexico Crips?

WINK: Suppose so.

MIR: You was in a Crips Gang?

WINK: Yes sir—Yes.

MIR: I read bout Crips. Mean.

WINK: They killed some folks.

MIR: You kill folks?

WINK: No sa ... No.

MIR: Help kill some?

WINK: Not yet.

MIR: What's "not yet" mean?

WINK: I was supposed to. Initiation.

MIR: Kill a human being to get initiated?

WINK: But I didn't.

MIR: But you was about to.

WINK: No hard plans.

MIR: But you wanted to initiate someday?

WINK: Suppose so.

 (Audio: CB: Luba: "Phyllis? This is Luba. Boys didn't say nothing about you cooking 'em lunch. Sorry. I'm out.")

 (Audio: CB: Phyllis: "It's fine. I got rhubarb pie if you want some. I'm out."

 (Audio: CB: Luba: "Sounds good. I'm out."

MIR: Whose idea to send you to this snow-blown chunk of ice?

WINK: Officer Sanchez asked Judge Endicott to order me here. Said Alaska could rehabilitate me.

MIR: Rehabilitate you? Me rehabilitate you?

 (WINK shrugs)

MIR: And why did Officer Sanchez or Judge whatever not ask me if I know how to rehabilitate a near-Tucson-violent Crips member?

 (WINK shrugs)

MIR: Quit shrugging your shoulders and look me in the eye when I ask you something.

WINK: Yes. I'll try to do that.

MIR: Do better than try.

WINK: I will.

EDDIE: May I use your facilities, please sir?

MIR: You dropped off your package. Go home.

EDDIE: Wind picked up. Can't fly out.

MIR: My rotten luck.

EDDIE: I'll bunk at the clinic.

MIR: For God sakes, I don't bite.

EDDIE: The CHR worker at the clinic won't set foot in your house. Said you bite.

MIR: CHR worker? Joannie? Now there's a lady with fangs. Scares the pants off me.

EDDIE: So may I use your—

MIR: —Eddie, you know damn well where the shit pot is.

   (EDDIE exits into hallway)

WINK: You two know one another?

MIR: When Eddie was a teenager, I taught him how to fish, hold a gun. Still can't shoot worth spit.

WINK: He acted like he didn't know you.

MIR: When the sun eclipses and Eddie finally gets a official assignment, suddenly he's "Trooper Caulfield." A flag man. Walks around acting official like he has a thorn up his ass. A real pain. He'll come back to normal soon as I feed him.

WINK: Spaghetti?

MIR: Halibut or salmon.

WINK: What's halibut?

MIR: Good Lord. What they make fish sticks out of. You've eaten fish sticks, ain't ya?

WINK: Little fish.

MIR: Big fish. Sometimes a hundred pound or more. People chop them into little fish sticks.

WINK: I don't eat fish.

MIR: No fish!? On account you live in a Arizona desert?

WINK: Fish stink.

MIR: Old fish stink. Fresh fish don't.

(Audio: CB: Matthew: "Walter? This is Matthew. Are my Xtratufs over there?")

(Audio: CB: Walter: "I give 'em to Billy to bring to ya. He wore 'em outta here. I'm out.")

(Audio: CB: Matthew: "God almighty. Who knows where my boots'll end up? I'm out.")

WINK: Does everyone here broadcast their personal business?

MIR: All day and night. No telephones except the clinic and school.

WINK: So you're supposed to be my grandpa or something?

MIR: What'd Trooper Caulfield and that Arizona Judge tell you?

WINK: Said you were my only living biological relative.

MIR: Biologic. I'd hardly call me "living." You sense anything familiar about Kodiak Island? The village?

WINK: No … Did you really not know I was coming?

MIR: I read the letter. Don't like helping Eddie when he's acting like a asshole. How long did you travel to get here?

WINK: A plane from Tucson to Phoenix, one to Seattle, one to Anchorage, one to Kodiak, and that little putt-putt plane to here. What's the name of this place?

MIR: Home.

WINK: The name of "home."

MIR: The village.

WINK: Like it's listed on the map.

MIR: Point Moser.

WINK: That plane from Kodiak to Point Moser was scary.

MIR: Mail planes is scary. Barely stay up in the sky.

WINK: Flying over rocks and snow and ocean and shit.

MIR: That's Kodiak Island. Rocks and snow and ocean and shit. See any whales? Bears?

WINK: I was too scared to look. Why do you call it a mail plane?

MIR: Since James, the pilot, added two big snow tires underneath, plane looks like it has testicles.

WINK: Sick.

MIR: It delivers our mail. No roads to the village or anywhere within a hundred mile.

WINK: Your mail plane was full of cases of beer.

MIR: Our usual mail: beer and whiskey.

WINK: Three cases of Lord Calvert.

MIR: Cheap whiskey. Once in a while there's a letter or two. Groceries.

WINK: You get groceries mailed by plane?

MIR: Mostly we hook or shoot food. Store-bought food comes on the mail plane. I radio the grocery store in Kodiak; they toss 'em on the mail plane.

WINK: Cool. *(Pause)* You live here alone?

MIR: Thirteen years. Peace and quiet. But the village is growing. Noisy. I have a piece of land up Olga Bay. Saving up to move there. Ain't a single soul around. Make it my fish camp. Peace and quiet. Where I can finish my life.

WINK: Thirteen years. Huh … My social worker, Ms. Marquez, said I was taken from here, from my family thirteen years ago. I was three.

MIR: You want some halibut?

WINK: You got more Chef-Boyardee?

MIR: I'll heat a can.

EDDIE: (*Enters buckling his belt*) Well, I feel a lot better.

MIR: Want some halibut? Anastasia dropped off a casserole.

EDDIE: Fantastic. Sure. You're in for a treat, Wink. Anastasia's halibut casserole is the best on the island.

WINK: What's in it?

MIR: Stinky fish.

EDDIE: Halibut, topped with mayo, spices, toasted in the oven.

WINK: Spaghetti sounds premium.

EDDIE: Spaghetti ain't natural.

WINK: You don't have to shoot or kill spaghetti.

EDDIE: Real food is shot or killed. Sure you was in them Crips?

(WINK shrugs)

MIR: Eddie? Fetch me a can of spaghetti from the pantry while I heat up your "premium" fish.

EDDIE: Sure thing, Mir.

(He exits into hallway)

WINK: You were right. Offer to feed the trooper and he turns normal. He was totally unfriendly on that roller-coaster plane ride.

MIR: Eddie hates planes. Turns his knuckles white. Hates boats more. Gets seasick. Projectile vomiting from stern to bow.

WINK: Rough.

(Audio: CB: Dustin: "This is Dustin. I'm missing a case of beer from today's plane. Anybody know anything, please let me know. I'm out.")

EDDIE: *(Entering)* Here you go. I popped it open.

MIR: Put it on the oil stove for our desert-minded guest.

WINK: With paper still on the can? It'll catch fire.

MIR: It does.

WINK: Burn down the place.

MIR: That happens too.

WINK: I hate fires.

MIR: *(Suddenly interested)* Why?

WINK: Give me nightmares.

MIR: Like what?

WINK: Like I'm burning.

MIR: Let me see your left elbow.

   (He grabs WINK'S left arm)

WINK: Don't touch me! I got burns on both elbows. Both knees.

MIR: Touchy.

   (He goes to stove and stirs spaghetti)

MIR: Why do you have burns on all four knees and elbows?

   (WINK shrugs)

MIR: Top secret?

WINK: *(Embarrassed)* Shit happens.

MIR: Shit that just happened or you made happen?

WINK: I don't ask you personal questions.

MIR: My house. I ask what I damn please ... You look like the inquiring type. Warning: don't.

WINK: May I be excused to use your "shit pot?"

MIR: Help yourself.

   (WINK exits into hallway)

EDDIE: *(Yells)* It probably stinks like a dead seal in there! *(To MIR)* I dropped a bomb in the nooshnik. What the hell was that about? "Warning: don't."

MIR: Nothing.

EDDIE: Afraid he'll learn your house burned?

MIR: Which year? Which house?

EDDIE: When your wife—

MIR: —Drop it! Or you can go wait out the storm in the clinic and let Joannie blab you to death.

EDDIE: Gee Mir. Thought you was over … Sorry.

MIR: That kid's not my grandson.

EDDIE: Get to know him.

MIR: He don't look like us. Don't smell like us.

EDDIE: He's been eating Arizona fast food and crap.

MIR: A government lady social worker pried my grandson from my arms. Kidnapped him when he had just turned three. Dragged him to the lower 48, changed his name, changed who he thought he was. Frigging made him into somebody else. Now they send this "Wink" kid up here, passing him off as Pavel.

EDDIE: Pavel? That was Wink's name?

MIR: My real grandson's name, retard. And now, like a frigging used-car salesman, sent me a car with four flat tires: foster homes, jails, lunatic asylums, church schools. You know what happened to little native kids in church schools? I lived in one of 'em when I was five.

EDDIE: Sexual stuff?

MIR: (*Looking sick*) That's where they sent Pavel. Where this other kid Wink's been. He's damaged goods. We was all sent back home damaged goods.

EDDIE: Maybe you can repair him.

MIR: You don't repair four flat tires. Even his spare tire is flat. A gang who kills people. He burns his self. God, Eddie. He burns his self.

EDDIE: You do okay, Mir.

MIR: Meaning what?

EDDIE: You lived in a church school. Served jail time.

MIR: Five days twice. Not for frigging killing people. Not for initiation rites and Mexican devil worshipping. I want him outta here, Eddie. Return him to his desert. To his Crips.

EDDIE: He's not a car you can send back.

MIR: He's adult now. Growed up. A human being I didn't ask for.

EDDIE: Teach him hunting and fishing. You taught me.

MIR: Lotta good that did.

EDDIE: You're getting old. You need help doing things.

MIR: He don't even eat frigging little fish sticks.

(WINK enters and sits)

WINK: Give me a frigging, crappy little fish stick. I'll eat ONE. *(Pouting)* God!

(Audio: CB: Luba: "This is Luba. Anyone got any white vinegar? I'm out.")

MIR: *(Embarrassed)* You uh … I didn't really mean—

WINK: —Yeah you did.

MIR: *(Pause)* Did you find everything you needed?

WINK: To take a shit? Thanks for asking … I couldn't get the toilet to stop running after I flushed it.

MIR: I keep it running so pipes don't freeze.

WINK: Wastes water.

MIR: We got water. This ain't the desert.

WINK: Fine.

(Audio: CB: Rena: "This is Rena. I got vinegar. I'm out."

EDDIE: Well, maybe I should take a rain check—snow check on that halibut casserole. You two need quality time alone. Get to know one another.

(WINK and MIR remain silent)

EDDIE: Don't uh … Don't shoot one another.

(EDDIE exits as MIR silently places bowl and spoon in front of WINK and sits)

(Audio: CB: Yvonne: "Dustin? This is Yvonne. We must got your extra case. I'm out.")

(WINK watches MIR eat with spoon, shrugs, shuffles to stove, grabs hold of can, immediately is burned, and releases can.)

WINK: Ouch!

(He pulls shirt sleeve over hand to pick up can and carry it to table. He stares at MIR eating spaghetti with a spoon.)

(Audio: CB: Dustin: "Appreciate it, Yvonne. I'm out.")

(WINK pours spaghetti into bowl and eats with spoon. MIR and WINK make no eye contact as they slurp and eat.)

(Lights: Fade to black)

End of Scene

Ahulaqs
Scene Two

Setting: Day. WINK is lying on couch watching TV with sound turned down while MIR is talking into CB.

MIR: Eddie. Come in Eddie. This is Mir. *(Pause)* Eddie. Come in Eddie. This is Mir. *(Pause)* Anyone know where State Trooper Edward Caulfield is?

(Audio: CB: Anastasia: "Cama'i Mir. This is Anastasia. Eddie went with Willie to hunt deer. I'm out.")

MIR: Thanks Anastasia. I'm out.

(Audio: CB: Walter: "Cama'i Mir. This is Walter. I think they went up Dead Man's Bay.")

MIR: Anyone flying today?

(Audio: CB: Walter: "Strong Southwest blow over Kodiak. Ceiling's down to a hundred. No one in or out today. Not even Anchorage to Kodiak. I'm out.")

MIR: Thanks Walter. I'm out. *(To Wink)* Want some coffee?

WINK: No thanks.

(MIR sits, heaps four spoons of sugar into coffee, and then adds excessive canned cream as WINK watches)

WINK: Four spoons of sugar and half a can of cream?

MIR: Don't like the taste of coffee.

WINK: Do you have diabetes?

(MIR opens Twinkie and eats it)

WINK: That's breakfast? Sugar, cream, and a Twinkie?

MIR: Year after year.

WINK: Damn.

MIR: What do you eat for breakfast?

WINK: Corn tortillas.

MIR: What the hell's that?

WINK: Thin, rolled pancakes. Filled with cheese, avocado, chopped tomatoes, peppers, black beans, spicy salsa. Drink grapefruit juice or plain tea.

MIR: Desert food. *(Eating Twinkie)* Love these things.

WINK: Did you hook or shoot your Twinkie?

MIR: *(Holding up remote control)* Want me to turn up the TV sound? We won't have to hear each other.

WINK: *(Looking at TV)* Those shows are stupid.

MIR: It's television.

WINK: You only get one channel.

MIR: We sort of get more than one channel.

WINK: One channel is one channel. It can't be "sort of more." And it's black and white.

MIR: The village only gets RAT NET.

WINK: What's that?

MIR: Alaska State TV. The state controls what we watch. Pumps one channel out to villages. Mix some ABC, some NBC, some CBS, some PBS, some local.

WINK: Totally weird.

MIR: We see previews all day long for shows that never show up.

WINK: *(Mumbling)* Censorship.

MIR: What great, fantastic shows are you missing due to having freedom of channels snatched from you?

WINK: MTV.

MIR: What's that?

WINK: Something you sure would never watch.

MIR: I almost never watch TV.

WINK: You watch news and weather.

MIR: I watch weather.

WINK: Boring.

MIR: Listen to Salmonberry Jam.

WINK: To what?

MIR: Music. AM radio.

WINK: AM radio. Right.

MIR: What do you do to not be bored? Other than kill people for initiation?

WINK: Stuff.

MIR: Stuff.

    (Audio: CB: Matthew: "Billy? This is Matthew. Where are you with my Xtratufs? I'm out.")

MIR: *(Holding up medication vial)* Are these your drugs?

WINK: Where did you get that?

MIR: Your pants pocket. When I sorted whites from coloreds.

WINK: I do my own wash.

MIR: High on drugs?

WINK: Those are medications.

MIR: Look like drugs.

WINK: I need them for nerves.

MIR: Do you know how many people the Coast Guard lifted out of this village cause of nerve pills? How many died?

WINK: My doctor prescribes them. They ain't the bad kind of—

MIR: —Never are. Nerve pills is always the good kind. I'll lock them in the safe with my insulin syringes. Let me know when your nerves cry out for your good kind of pills.

WINK: I need my pills! They're the real deal.

MIR: No doubt.

WINK: You can't take them away.

MIR: Watch.

(He locks medicine bottle in small safe as WINK pouts, growing anxious)

WINK: What drugs do you take?

MIR: I don't take drugs. I take absolutely necessary medications.

WINK: "Absolutely necessary."

MIR: Absolutely.

WINK: What other than insulin is "absolutely necessary?"

MIR: My business.

WINK: Top secret?

MIR: Blood pressure.

WINK: Bet I'm helping your blood pressure, huh?

MIR: It's doing fair.

WINK: Pain pills?

MIR: Nope.

WINK: Nerve pills?

MIR: Nope.

WINK: Ginseng?

MIR: What's that?

WINK: Aphrodisiac.

MIR: It's clear you haven't been in a village. Or been my age.

WINK: I met a Mexican guy who was 73. His wife and girlfriend were both pregnant by him.

MIR: Bet the ladies weren't 73.

WINK: Lord Calvert?

MIR: Nope.

WINK: Beer?

MIR: Nope.

WINK: Wine?

MIR: Nope. No Gin. No rum. No fancy liqueurs. No rubbing alcohol. Not even mouthwash.

WINK: Mouthwash?

MIR: We had a guy living here, second cousin. Mixed lighter fluid with milk to get high. Called it, "Fire Milk."

WINK: That's wicked.

MIR: Died of liver failure.

WINK: Damn … Weed?

MIR: Nope. No weed. No cocaine. No LSD. Have baby aspirin. Good for circulation.

WINK: How about other villagers?

MIR: Everything you want or don't want.

WINK: You ever want anything?

MIR: Every day. I've been clean thirteen years. Ever since … Thirteen years.

WINK: Top secret.

MIR: How long have you been clean?

WINK: According to your perceptions? I've been clean since you locked my medications in your frigging safe. So, ten minutes.

MIR: Other stuff.

WINK: Top secret.

MIR: Fair enough.

(Audio: CB: Matthew: "Has anyone, anywhere seen Billy? He's got my boots. I'm out.")

(Audio: CB: Yvonne: "Matthew? This is Yvonne. I seen Billy passed out at Art's place. I'm out.")

(Audio: CB: Matthew: "Appreciate it, Yvonne. I'm out.")

WINK: You ever been in jail?

MIR: Stupid stuff.

WINK: That's what everybody locked up says.

MIR: Really stupid stuff.

WINK: How stupid?

MIR: My wife, Alyona, and I tied one on. A ritual back then.

WINK: Beer?

MIR: Lord Calvert. Five, six-day drunk. Alyona had an abscess tooth. Nasty rotten tooth. Terrible pain. Lord Calvert helped. We could hardly stand, walk. She screamed how her tooth hurt. "It's killing me, Mir. Killing me." I pinned her down on top of that kitchen table, grabbed my pliers, yanked it out.

WINK: Holy shit.

MIR: She passed out. Then I passed out. Fifteen, sixteen hours later, we woke. I had yanked out the wrong tooth.

WINK: Oh my God.

MIR: Her mother called the state troopers. I spent five nights in the slammer.

WINK: Holy shit.

MIR: Perfectly good tooth. Roots and all. Stupid stuff.

WINK: Premium stupid. *(Pause)* Other stuff?

MIR: Top secret.

WINK: Fair. Fair enough.

(Audio: CB: Anastasia: "Mir? Hey Mir, you on this one?")

MIR: *(To CB)* This is Mir. Go ahead.

(Audio: CB: Anastasia: "Got a fresh pot of deer stew if you boys want some. How's your grandson doing?"

MIR: I'll be over to get stew. Quyanaa. My visitor's learning village ways. I'm out.

(He hangs up CB. WINK slams down remote control and exits into hallway.)

End of Scene

Ahulaqs
Scene Three

Setting: Morning. WINK is lying on the couch reading a book while MIR cleans the kitchen.

MIR: Sure you don't want anything for breakfast?

WINK: Twinkies and sweet muddy coffee?

MIR: *(Putting on coat)* I'm walking to the clinic to see if my insulin came in.

WINK: I thought mail planes couldn't get in or out.

MIR: It could have come on your plane a few days back. You need anything, use the CB. It'll reach the clinic or friends' houses.

WINK: I thought you didn't have friends.

(MIR exits outside while WINK continues reading.)

(Audio: CB: Luba: "David? Willie? This is Luba. You two eating breakfast over here with us? We got alaciqs. I'm out.")

(Audio: CB: Willie: "This is Willie. Quyanaa. We had Fruit Loops at Grandma's. I'm out.")

(EDDIE enters vestibule, pulls off coat, and opens inner door)

EDDIE: Morning. Mir said you was awake.

WINK: You didn't knock. Guess this ain't official business.

EDDIE: Just wanted to say hello.

WINK: *(Putting down book)* Come the rest of the way in.

EDDIE: Think I'll help myself to some coffee. You want any?

WINK: Just black.

EDDIE: I like mine suffocated with cream and sugar.

WINK: Like most of the village. Are you diabetic too?

EDDIE: It's under control. You two feeling each other out? Learning one another's secrets?

WINK: Mir don't talk much. Except to complain. If I ask questions, he grinds his dentures.

EDDIE: He's suffered lots over the years. Keeps it close to his chest.

WINK: Like what?

EDDIE: Here's your coffee. Don't know how you can stand it black. You trying to use me as your spy?

WINK: Ain't gonna learn from Mir.

EDDIE: You got memories of growing up here?

WINK: Joannie said I was turning three when Troopers took me.

EDDIE: Up north, the Yupik word for Trooper is, "someone who takes people away." My most unfavorite assignment.

WINK: I don't remember nothing before six or seven. I was bounced home to home before I remember anything.

EDDIE: Seems like something would be familiar. Alitek Mountain, the church, banyas, something.

WINK: "Nope." Mir's favorite word: "Nope."

EDDIE: Well, you didn't grow up in this house, even if you is his grandson.

WINK: Which house did I allegedly grow up in?

EDDIE: Your house burned. Only a few things in your bedroom survived. Pictures of you, your grandparents, your mom, all burned up. You almost burned up.

WINK: I almost burned to death?

EDDIE: Story goes your grandma saved you. She and Mir was next door at Lawrence and Nina's. Someone out in the street yelled "fire." Your grandma ran through the flames, wrapped you in a blanket, tossed you out the window.

WINK: Brave lady.

EDDIE: Your elbow got burned.

WINK: That's why Mir checked my elbow.

EDDIE: They say it was a nasty burn. Weather was bad. Planes couldn't get in and out. Village clinic didn't have much back then. Your infection grew worse. Miracle you made it.

WINK: And my grandma?

EDDIE: *(Pause)* You don't know?

   (WINK shakes his head)

EDDIE: *(Pause)* She died.

WINK: In the fire? That's how my grandma died?

EDDIE: People seen her through the window.

WINK: Saving me? Burning?

EDDIE: If you're their grandson.

WINK: Why Mir hates me.

EDDIE: He doesn't hate you. It weren't your fault. Your grandparents left you alone in that old wooden house. A three-year old.

WINK: I feel sick.

EDDIE: They should have been looking after you.

   (Audio: CB: Matthew: "Luba? This is Matthew. Billy come to yet?")

   (Audio: CB: Luba: "Yeah. He left with Phillip. I'm out.")

   (Audio: CB: Matthew: "Wearing my boots?")

   (Audio: CB: Luba: "Xtratufs. Maybe. I'm out.")

   (Audio: CB: Matthew: "I'm out.")

EDDIE: You remember any of that?

WINK: I get nightmares of fires.

   (EDDIE nods)

WINK: So, after my grandma died, I lived with Mir?

EDDIE: Walter and Rena's. Maybe a month. Then you was taken. At least what Anastasia told me. I never asked more … Don't tell Mir I told you.

WINK: I don't speak to Mir about nothing.

EDDIE: You should talk about everything.

WINK: He hates me. I feel it in my bones.

EDDIE: He's getting old. Nothing personal to do with you.

(ANASTASIA enters vestibule and knocks)

EDDIE: Come in!

WINK: I'm supposed to say that.

EDDIE: Say it.

WINK: *(Yells)* Come in!

ANASTASIA: *(Entering)* Hi boys.

EDDIE: Hi Anastasia. Have you met Wink?

ANASTASIA: Seen him asleep on the couch when I dropped off halibut.

WINK: *(Stands)* You must think I'm rude, sleeping through your visit. I apologize.

ANASTASIA: Young people keep different hours than old people. It's fine, Wink. You go by "Wink," right?

WINK: Yeah. I don't claim, "Robert."

ANASTASIA: Why do they call you, "Wink?"

WINK: When I was nine or so, the foster home I was in, whenever my foster father, Rich, made a joke at the expense of Joyce, my foster mother, Rich looked at me to see if I got his joke. If I did, I gave Rich a little wink. Like this.

(He winks)

ANASTASIA: So, your foster dad named you.

WINK: Actually, Joyce did. She saw my reflection in her kitchen window, in her shiny pots. She named me.

ANASTASIA: I would like Joyce.

WINK: She was cool.

ANASTASIA: Why didn't you stay there?

WINK: They were temporary parents. Traded kids every six months.

ANASTASIA: Moving babies and children around every six months. What a world.

WINK: They were my favorite. The other homes ... not.

ANASTASIA: So many of us. *(Pause)* Didn't mean to interrupt what you and Edward was talking about.

EDDIE: Weather.

WINK: Planes.

ANASTASIA: Weather and planes. Most of our lives: weather and planes.

EDDIE: Matter of fact, I was just going. Just dropped in for a cup. Got reports to fill out.

ANASTASIA: Don't leave on my account.

EDDIE: No. Nothing like that.

WINK: Eddie doesn't want to offend you and not get more halibut.

EDDIE: Not true. I mean ... I wouldn't offend Anastasia ever. She's one great woman.

ANASTASIA: Go fill out your reports, Edward. Leave me and this fine young man to talk.

EDDIE: Uh ... Sure.

    (He puts on coat and exits outside as ANASTASIA slides casserole into oven)

ANASTASIA: You understand Trooper Caulfield well for such a short time in the village.

WINK: He's a good guy. When he's not acting official.

ANASTASIA: You seen "official," did you? Pretty comical.

WINK: Like Barney Fife.

ANASTASIA: Barney who?

WINK: Barney Fife. Andy Griffith Show reruns. On your one-channel TV. Squeezed in between President Reagan speeches and weather.

ANASTASIA: Anything you like about the village?

WINK: Your halibut.

ANASTASIA: Mir said you don't eat fish.

WINK: I sneaked a taste. Don't tell him.

ANASTASIA: Stubborn. You gotta be Mir's grandson.

WINK: Why doesn't he like my name?

ANASTASIA: Wink?

WINK: Robert.

ANASTASIA: That weren't your name when you lived here.

WINK: "Robert" was always my name.

ANASTASIA: They renamed you when they took you down to Oregon or Idaho. So we was told.

WINK: Renamed me? No one ever told me … What was my real name?

ANASTASIA: Pavel. Like many of us. Russian names.

WINK: Not Aleut?

ANASTASIA: The Government renamed our people back in the 1920s. Traded our Aleut names for Russian names. After the 1700's sea otter hunts and fur trading, there were way too many Russians living here, *(pointing out window)* building Russian Orthodox Churches like that one.

(Audio: CB: Grandma Phyllis: "Anastasia? This is Phyllis. You coming for coffee?")

ANASTASIA: Pardon me a moment. *(Into CB)* Phyllis? Be there in a bit. Talking with Wink. I'm out.

(Audio: CB: Grandma Phyllis: "Okay. I'm out.")

ANASTASIA: We pretty much lost our language. A few words hold on like greetings, farewells, plant names. Not much.

WINK: What was my mother's name?

ANASTASIA: Mir doesn't talk to you.

(WINK shakes his head)

ANASTASIA: Your mother was a beautiful woman. Dark native skin like your Grandma Alyona. Not pale Russian skin like Mir. She was striking.

WINK: What was her name?

ANASTASIA: Galina.

WINK: Galina … That's beautiful … What about my father?

ANASTASIA: Big mystery.

WINK: You don't know?

ANASTASIA: Galina kept secret your father's name. There was lots of ugly gossip, of course. Some said your father was Wilson Mathers, young Aleut boy sometimes visiting from Old Harbor. He also had beautiful dark native skin.

WINK: What was the worse gossip?

ANASTASIA: Stuff I don't repeat.

WINK: That's not fair to me.

ANASTASIA: People spread terrible rumors in villages.

WINK: Old men having sex with young girls?

ANASTASIA: Where on earth did you hear such a thing?

WINK: Happened places I lived. Church schools. Foster homes.

ANASTASIA: Not just villages, I guess.

(WINK shrugs)

ANASTASIA: Well, let's you and me not join folks spreading such rot.

WINK: Fair enough … Did my mom say anything about my dad? Anything at all?

ANASTASIA: Galena was evasive. Took after Mir. Once, she shared with me there was a fisherman, probably a cannery worker down at Alitak who passed through the village one night, and she and he, well, she claimed to me, he was your father. Never spoke his name. Nothing about his background. She was proud to have you. Show you off to everyone. Wore that pride on her face. Bragged you were only "half heathen."

WINK: What's that mean?

ANASTASIA: School teachers used to wash our mouths out with soap and call us heathens and make us stand in the classroom corner all day long if we slipped and said even one Aleut word in class. Only allowed English in school.

WINK: And at home?

ANASTASIA: Aleut. But slowly over the years, that's disappeared.

WINK: What happened to my mother?

ANASTASIA: You can't tell Mir I told you this stuff.

WINK: I don't tell him nothing.

ANASTASIA: He would be mad at me.

WINK: I promise.

ANASTASIA: May I have a cup of coffee? Black?

WINK: *(Jumping up to get coffee)* Black? Absolutely.

ANASTASIA: Your mother was the best fisherman in the village—This end of Kodiak. Mir wanted a son, but Mir and Alyona never had a second child. So, Mir taught Galena to fish. Raised her like a son. Also, a keen hunter. Like many young village people, Galena began drinking. We lost many young people going out fishing when drunk. Last year, three boys went out in a skiff, hunting sea lion out at Geese Channel. Never come home.

WINK: My mother never came home?

(Audio: CB: Dustin: "This is Dustin. We collected some uutuks if anyone wants some. I'm out.")

ANASTASIA: She and Mir was fishing up Dead Man's Bay. Winter. Dark at four pm. They had always been careful to get back before sunset but that night? It must have been one, two in the morning when Mir's skiff pulled in. Come back using the light of his flashlight. Alone.

WINK: What did he say?

ANASTASIA: Typical Mir style. Said nothing. For days he said nothing. When State Troopers come down, Mir said he and Galena had went ashore cause waves was choppy, and they wanted to clean their fish on shore. So, they drank some, cleaned some, drank more, cleaned more. He told troopers he was putting cleaned salmon and halibut into the skiff, could barely hear over choppy water splashing against the skiff, when he heard Galena scream. Said something was pulling her through the brush up the ridge.

WINK: A bear?

ANASTASIA: Walking on hind legs.

(Audio: CB: Yvonne: "This is Yvonne. I'll be over to get some. Quyanaa. I'm out.")

WINK: What could do that?

ANASTASIA: Ahulaq.

WINK: What's Ahulaq?

ANASTASIA: Old, stupid Aleut ghost story.

WINK: So, they're not real?

ANASTASIA: Never say that around village people. They believe in Ahulaqs.

WINK: What are they?

ANASTASIA: Kind of like Bigfoot or those Abominable Snowman overseas, wherever stories say they live.

WINK: Himalayas.

ANASTASIA: Almost everybody here has seen Ahulaqs one time or another. Far off in the snow, through the brush, top of the mountains. Big tracks. Big as Kodiak Bear tracks, but the shape of human footprints. They're covered with long dirty brown hair, but faces more like humans.

WINK: Do they wear clothes?

ANASTASIA: Long hair keeps them warm like any animal. Sometimes they cry out. Wolf sounds. Howling. More mournful.

WINK: Do they come into the village?

ANASTASIA: Some say Ahulaqs come close to fetch young women to keep their kind breeding. Keeps young women close to the village, close to our men. Maybe that's the reason for the story. Like I said, don't say anything that sounds like you don't believe.

WINK: What would happen?

ANASTASIA: Most of us never tell outsiders about Ahulaqs. Don't want to be ridiculed. Ahulaq stories are sacred, part of our culture. We don't need more of our culture disappearing cause of white people.

> *(Audio: CB: Steve: "This is Steve at the school. Gym will be open for public volleyball three to five today and again tonight. I'm out.")*

WINK: I won't say a word.

ANASTASIA: You're smart, Wink. Or Robert. Or Pavel. A good heart. I pray you stay here.

WINK: I don't know I can.

ANASTASIA: You didn't know you could eat fish.

WINK: Not publicly.

ANASTASIA: *(Laughing)* Push past your stubbornness.

WINK: Do people believe Mir that the Ahulaq took my mother?

ANASTASIA: My oh my. Some believe they got into a drunken brawl. Maybe fell overboard. Others believe Mir shoved her. When they got drunk, they was stubborn as stubborn gets. Ferocious arguments. Once, they disagreed how to cook reindeer sausage. Galina clobbered Mir over the head with a cast-iron fry pan.

(MIR enters vestibule, pulls off coat and boots, and enters inside)

MIR: Looks like you found another victim to listen to your gossip.

ANASTASIA: This boy has a big heart.

MIR: Mind your own business, Anastasia.

WINK: She's our guest.

MIR: My house. I say what I want.

ANASTASIA: Always have, Mir.

MIR: What craziness did you fill this boy's head with?

WINK: Ahulaqs.

MIR: Christ almighty.

WINK: Have you seen one?

MIR: Ages ago. Another life.

WINK: Where?

MIR: I don't discuss Ahulaqs.

WINK: Can you just tell me where so I can—

MIR: —I don't talk about Ahulaqs!

WINK: *(To ANASTASIA)* Told you he hates me.

MIR: I don't know you well enough to hate. You have to be close to people to love and hate.

ANASTASIA: I put halibut in the oven, ready to eat.

MIR: This one don't eat fish.

ANASTASIA: Maybe he'll try a taste. It's my best.

(*She enters vestibule and puts on coat*)

ANASTASIA: I'll see you two soon.

MIR: I would appreciate if you don't talk to Wink when I'm not around.

(*Audio: CB: Grandma Phyllis: "Anastasia? Phyllis. Still got coffee on the stove. I'm out."*)

ANASTASIA: Wanted to be welcoming.

MIR: Only when I'm around. Understand?

ANASTASIA: (*Pause*) I understand years and years of stubbornness.

(*She winks at WINK and he winks back*)

MIR: What was that? You two winking.

ANASTASIA: How this boy got his nickname. Ask him sometime. (*Exiting outside*) When you ain't being so all fired stubborn.

MIR: That woman drives me crazy.

WINK: You like her fish.

MIR: Big price to pay for a bite of good fish. What'd you two talk about?

WINK: Ahulaqs.

MIR: Anything else?

WINK: How I won't stay much longer in Point Moser.

MIR: You don't settle long nowhere, do you? Don't stick with nothing long.

WINK: What do you mean?

MIR: I read your report. Dropped out of school. Ran away from the hospital. Quit all jobs within a couple of days. Float in the wind house to house, person to person. It's better you leave here. You're not my grandson.

WINK: You kicking me out?

MIR: I never invited you. Go back to your Crips.

WINK: Crips was like family. Fed me. Gave me places to sleep. Taught me more than any school book. The women in the Crips was more like mothers than any foster mother or church nun. They loved me. Honest love.

MIR: You shouldn't had left 'em. What trouble did you get in that you had to leave?

(WINK shrugs)

MIR: Weed?

(WINK shrugs)

MIR: Jail time. Must have been more than "weed."

WINK: You served jail time. I heard you tell Eddie.

MIR: You have no right eavesdropping. That's my business, you little asshole.

WINK: Oh. You can ask about me, read my report, but I can't know who I am living with, sleeping in a house with.

MIR: What's sleeping in this house got to do with anything?

WINK: You know what happened to my mother.

MIR: Damn that gossiping bitch.

WINK: She said my mother was beautiful. Dark native skin. Loved me. That you took her out fishing when you was drunk, and she never came back, and you won't tell anybody what happened.

MIR: *(Screams)* I want you out of here! Understand, you fucker!?

WINK: I understand too well.

(He rushes through vestibule and outside)

MIR: Take your crap coat with you!

WINK: *(Off stage, yelling back)* What do you care?

(MIR *slams outside door and then the inside door. He paces, goes to cabinet, tosses papers, glasses, cups, etc. onto floor from lower cabinet, pulls out an unopened whiskey bottle, sets it on counter, paces, looks back at it, away from it, repeating this pattern several times. He sits on couch staring at bottle, and then yells at bottle.)*

MIR: You ain't gonna take me over! Not after thirteen years. God!

(He gets up, paces, grabs bottle, opens it, paces with bottle in hand, and starts to take drink.)

MIR: No! *(Getting down on knees)* No. No. No.

(He starts to take drink, gets up, and kneels beside couch with bottle still in hand)

MIR: Please God help me. I can't do this. Not alone.

(He stares at bottle, drinks several large gulps of whiskey, pauses, drinks several more gulps, leans on couch, covers head with arms, and sobs.)

(Audio: CB: Dustin: "This is Dustin. We're having a birthday party at lunch tomorrow. Michella turns four. Everyone's invited. Bring your own. I'm out.")

End of Scene

Ahulaqs
Scene Four

Setting: Evening on same day. Dark outside. MIR is asleep on couch. He wakes with a hangover and looks at watch. He stumbles around house looking for WINK and panics when he cannot find him.

MIR: Shit.

(He hurries to the CB)

MIR: Eddie. Eddie. Got a emergency. Come in Eddie. *(Pause)* Wink's gone. Left the house five or six hours ago without his coat. Do you read me, Eddie? *(Pause)* Eddie? *(To self)* Damn!

(Audio: CB: Anastasia: "Mir? I seen Eddie outside the church. He found something and's headed your way carrying something big. I'm out.")

(MIR rushes to window and looks out for several seconds)

MIR: Oh God.

(He rushes to outside door and opens it. EDDIE enters carrying WINK wrapped in a blanket.)

MIR: Oh my God.

EDDIE: I found him half-buried in a drift without a stitch of clothing.

(EDDIE and MIR lay WINK on couch)

MIR: He's cold as an icicle.

EDDIE: He scattered his clothes across the field. Gotta be snow madness.

MIR: Grab coffee quick. Oh my God, Wink!

(As EDDIE pours coffee, MIR rubs WINK'S bare feet with his hands, breaths on his hands and rubs Wink's feet more)

MIR: Come on Wink. Hold on son. You can do it.

EDDIE: He wasn't even shivering. Thought he was dead.

MIR: *(Yells)* Bring the damn coffee! And another blanket! *(To Wink)* You hear me, boy? Open your eyes or move something. I should never have—Forget the blanket! Soak them dish rags in hot water. Warm his neck and armpits. I remember to do that for hypothermia. Get blood flowing in them areas. Hurry!

EDDIE: I am!

MIR: Heat 'em on the stove for Christ's sake!

EDDIE: *(Handing rags to MIR)* Your water's plenty hot.

(Audio: CB: Steve: "This is Steve. Reminder: public volleyball at school gym seven to nine tonight. I'm out.")

(MIR stuffs rags in WINK'S arm pits and around his neck)

EDDIE: Supposed to do the groin too.

MIR: Don't just stand there watching!

(EDDIE wets another rag and reaches under blanket to add it to WINK'S groin)

MIR: My God he's frozen.

EDDIE: He moved.

MIR: I didn't see it.

(WINK makes small movement)

EDDIE: There.

MIR: I seen it. I seen it. Wink? Wink?

(WINK makes another small movement and groans)

MIR: What the hell was you doing naked in the snow?

WINK: *(Eyes closed)* Huh?

MIR: You stripped off your clothes.

WINK: I don't ... Huh?

MIR: Liked to froze to death.

WINK: Hearing.

MIR: Hearing what?

WINK: Things.

MIR: What things?

(WINK turns away)

(Audio: CB: Anastasia): "Mir? Anastasia. If you guys need me or need Glenda from the clinic let me know. I'm out.")

MIR: It was your pills. I took away your pills, God damn it. Why didn't you tell me you had to have 'em?

WINK: You got mad.

MIR: God almighty, Wink. I didn't know them pills was important.

WINK: Uh huh.

MIR: I know that NOW ... What was you hearing?

(WINK remains silent)

MIR: I won't be mad. Cross my heart and hope to die.

(WINK remains silent)

MIR: I swear on that piece of land up in Olga Bay.

WINK: Voice.

MIR: Saying what?

WINK: Cussing.

MIR: Cussing what?

WINK: Names.

MIR: What names?

WINK: Don't make sense.

MIR: What names?

WINK: *(Pause)* "You flame throwing cunt."

MIR: What?

WINK: Over and over.

EDDIE: That's awful.

(MIR holds WINK, rocking him back and forth)

MIR: *(To EDDIE)* I used to yell that at his grandma. When we was drunk. Called her a "flame throwing cunt." She'd pass out smoking. Leave dish towels on the stove. Start fires. *(To WINK)* You was just two. That's my voice. Them words weren't never for you. I'll grab one'a yer pills.

(MIR hurries to safe, gets pill bottle, and then a glass of water)

MIR: How many?

WINK: One.

MIR: How fast do they work?

WINK: Day or two.

MIR: We gotta make 'em work faster. You can't have me in your head. Not them ugly words.

WINK: I'm scared.

MIR: Me too. Swallow this.

(WINK swallows pill)

MIR: Good. Sip more.

WINK: *(Sips)* It's warm.

MIR: Warm's good … You hearing the voice now?

(WINK nods. MIR cuddles him and rocks him more).

MIR: What's it saying?

WINK: Go back to the snow.

MIR: Oh God no. No Wink. Which way's that voice coming from?

WINK: There.

(He points behind the left of his head)

WINK: Always that way.

MIR: When you was little, and you was scared? You know what I did?

(WINK shakes his head "no")

MIR: You had a squirt gun. I still got it. Eddie! Grab me that puny squirt gun on the top shelf in my bedroom.

(EDDIE exits into hallway)

(Audio: CB: Glenda: "Mir? This is Glenda. Let me know if you need anything from the clinic. Or if I need to come over there. I'm out.")

MIR: You loved that stupid little squirt gun. Carried it everywhere. Only thing in your room survived the fire. You got scared there was Ahulaqs in the house. So, we laid on the couch, like you and me is doing now, but you was small. You was on my lap and shot 'em. Shot Ahulaqs with your little squirt gun.

WINK: Squirt gun?

MIR: Laughed every darn time. So hard laughing, you farted and spit up.

WINK: I shot 'em?

MIR: Never missed.

(EDDIE enters with squirt gun, gives it to MIR, and sits across the room)

(Lights: Dissolve from full room lights to only bright spots on WINK and MIR on the couch)

MIR: You was two. Half pint of a guy. Remember?

WINK: No.

MIR: Hold the gun in your hand. Finger the trigger. Now, when you hear that voice over your left shoulder, shoot it.

WINK: It won't help.

MIR: Do it.

(WINK shivers strongly as he sits up a bit)

MIR: Gosh you're cold. I'll warm you.

(He hugs WINK tighter and rubs his shoulders)

MIR: You heard him yet?

WINK: He scares me.

MIR: *(Gentle whisper)* Shoot him.

(WINK pauses and then shoots over left shoulder)

MIR: You got him.

WINK: Yeah?

MIR: Winged his right ear.

WINK: How do you know?

MIR: You hear him. I see him. Plain as day. We're a team. You listen. I look. The minute he starts cussing, let me know. I'll help you aim.

WINK: He's cussing.

MIR: Shoot up and left!

(WINK shoots left)

MIR: In the chin! Little higher next time. Blast his nose. Even better? Between his eyes. That really pisses him off.

WINK: I don't want to piss him off.

MIR: Yeah you do. Drive him out of our home.

WINK: What's he look like?

MIR: Well ... sounds like me, right? Saying what I used to say. Using my voice.

WINK: Like you.

MIR: He's tricky. But he looks like ... like them Ahulaqs.

WINK: What do they look like?

MIR: Kodiak Bear like. Not beautiful like Kodiaks. Ugly. Like my face pasted on a Kodiak.

WINK: You ain't ugly.

MIR: You ain't been looking close. Moment he cusses, shoot.

(WINK pauses and then shoots left)

MIR: Ooops. You wasn't careful. I know you're shivering with cold, but keep a steady aim. Shoot again.

WINK: You really see him?

MIR: Ugly bastard. Aim higher.

WINK: I can't see him.

MIR: I'm doing the looking. A little left and up.

(WINK pauses and shoots)

MIR: Between his eyes! Smack in the middle!

WINK: That's good, right?

MIR: Damn good. Now get ready. Piss him off with another fantastic Ivanov-type shot.

WINK: Ivanov.

(He pauses and then shoots)

MIR: Two in a row! Working together we're gonna fucking drive that beast back in them mountains. He ain't never gonna crawl back in our little warm home.

(WINK laughs mildly)

MIR: Oh, you think it's funny, huh? Me too.

(He hugs WINK tighter, tearful)

MIR: Me too, Wink. Me too.

(WINK releases gun and grabs MIR'S ring finger)

MIR: What you doing, Wink? Why you holding my finger? We got Ahulaqs to shoot.

(WINK remains silent)

MIR: Oh my God. Oh dear God. When you was two, almost three? You used to squeeze my ring finger like that. You remember?

(WINK shakes head "no")

MIR: Qilimaq. Aleut word for ring finger.

WINK: Qilimaq.

MIR: Your grandma Alyona taught us that word. Me and you both.

WINK: Qilimaq.

MIR: I used to spread newspapers on the floor. We'd make believe newspapers was yours and my ledge. Way high up on a cliff.

WINK: Volcano cliff.

MIR: Right. And you squeezed my ring finger tight so you wouldn't fall.

WINK: Fall in hot lava.

MIR: Hot lava. Right. Our secret volcano. Mount ... Mount ...

WINK: Mount Taquka'aq.

MIR: Mount Taquka'aq. Mount Bear. You remember, Wink.

WINK: Taquka'aq.

MIR: *(Hugging Wink tightly, rocking him)* I never once let you fall.

WINK: I can't hear the Ahulaq.

MIR: He's out there. As long as we keep that furry giant outside, drive that critter back into his mountains and cave, don't let him back inside us, we'll be fine, Mooqtuk. Fine.

WINK: I know, Appa.

MIR: Mooqtuk.

(MIR and WINK gently close eyes and relax)

(Audio: Artic wind increases howling outside)

(Lights: Dissolve from white spot lights on MIR and WINK to normal, full room lighting)

(EDDIE slowly walks to couch, looks at MIR and WINK, smiles, spreads another blanket over both MIR and WINK, puts on coat, and exits outside)

(Audio: CB: Matthew: "God almighty. This is Matthew. Has anyone seen Billy with my frigging boots? (Pause) Anyone? ... I'm out.")

(Lights: Fade to black)

(Audio: Wind continues for some time after lights fade)

FINALE

DC Fidler (Author)

A native of the North Carolina Appalachian Mountains, DC Fidler has combined a career in academic psychiatry and cultural psychiatry with a lifetime of playwriting, acting, directing, composing music, and teaching creative writing and the dramatic arts.

He studied theatre, writing, medicine, and psychiatry at the University of North Carolina at Chapel Hill, where he served on the faculty. He later served on the faculty at West Virginia University and also practiced psychiatry in Australia and New Zealand.

He began his acting career in outdoor dramas, summer stock theatre, and local films and television at age ten. He has written scripts and composed music for over fifty medical educational videos and his plays have been produced in community theatres, at universities, and in professional theatres in North Carolina, Virginia, Ohio, West Virginia, Alaska, St. Louis, Sacramento, San Diego, Los Angeles, Boston, Chicago, and New York City.

He consulted and appeared in educational productions for HBO, ABC, and PBS and performed in stage plays including: *Hope is the Thing with Feathers, Night of January 16th, Thieves' Carnival, Blood Wedding, Our Town, A Life in the Theatre*, and *Fool for Love*. DC Fidler is an active member of the Dramatists Guild of America and the Charlotte Writers' Club.

Fidler previously chaired the Video Committee for the American Psychiatric Association and served as President of the Association for Academic Psychiatry, promoting the use of arts in psychiatry. He was inducted as a Fellow of the Royal College of Physicians of Ireland and serves on the Arts and Humanities Committee for the Group for the Advancement of Psychiatry, co-producing a video series on the History of Psychiatry.

DC Fidler lived and worked with the Alutiiq tribe in Akhiok, Alaska, the Al Moqbali Bedouin tribe near Sohar, Oman, the Kalkadoon Tribe in the outback of Queensland, Australia, and the Te Tau Ihu Maori Tribes on the South Island of New Zealand.

He is author of the textbook, *Psychiatry for Actors: Building a Character Using Psychiatric Principles*, and author of the novels, *Boogieban* and *Wood Whisperers*.

Plays, Novels, and Textbooks by DC Fidler

Novels and Textbooks
- Boogieban
- Wood Whisperers
- Psychiatry for Actors: Building a Character Using Psychiatric Principles

Plays
- Voices in the Woods
- Guilt by Association (With RJ Casey)
- Three Diaries
- Sir William Bowlinggreen and Company
- Shiraz
- Anniversary of Miss Nanette Pringle
- School Children Hiding Under Desks
- Grams
- Camp Uni
- Boogieban (Two-Actor Version)
- Boogieban (Seven-Actor Version)
- Ahulaqs
- Elk and Wolf (With Travis Teffner)
- Santee Delta (With Travis Teffner)
- Celtic Crossing
- Stone Touchin'
- Daugherty Park Merry-Go-Round
- La Dynastie
- The Last Farm
- Gyges
- Begat

Short Plays
- Persons
- Cruise
- Mobile to Where

- Oman Truce
- Second Amendment
- The Greek God Club
- Five X
- Microscopic Misconceptions
- Drone Guns
- Moon Bugs (With Travis Teffner)

Screenplays
- Green Lights of Baghdad (with RJ Casey)

Musicals
- Pied Piper (With Lauren Horacek)
- Healer Man
- Medicine Show